ISBN: 9798742834151
Imprint: Independently published
Published by: La'Tosha Price
Pricelessstorytime@gmail.com
Edited by: Carlos Price
cprice1721@gmail.com
Illustrated by: La'Tosha Price

Introduction

    I'm a creator, a visionary, a playwright and a storyteller. I approach the world with the eyes of an artist, the ears of a musician, and the soul of a writer. I see the endless possibilities when others see only problems and obstacles. Musical plays, children's art museums, and my own children have been sources of inspiration to me, as well as gospel music and praise and worship. I value the importance of abandoning momentarily my adult wisdom and knowledge so that I can accurately tell a story about life through a child's eyes. I believe that quality is one of God's gifts to me.

    Another of His gifts to me is writing. I love to write! Maybe that's because words flow easily from my brain to my fingertips, and my heart beats rapidly with excitement as my efforts allow an idea to become a reality on the paper in front of me. No matter the time of night or day that I sit to focus upon writing, once the story is inside me, I have to tell it! If my family members are nearby, they must hear about what I'm thinking. And then the magic happens when I assume the mind of a child and present my story in written form.

    All children delight in reading stories about characters looking and acting like they do. However, for reasons of history, racism, economics and so much more, there are too few children's books where African-American kids like mine get to feel validated by the content of the stories they read. I felt compelled to take action by using my gifts to honor God and children together. So this book about a series of events in the life of "Jonah'" details incidences that happen to all children, but the faces of all the characters here are of persons of color.

    My goal is to spread the word about the power of accomplishing your dreams, and the excellence in reading that produces the power of knowledge! I learned to dream through reading, learned to create dreams through writing, and learned to develop dreamers through teaching. I shall always be a dreamer. Dreams really do come true, so I invite readers to come along and dream with me.

La'Tosha Price

(You know he woke me up this morning and I'm glad),
glad),
I'm glad about it,
(I'm so glad), I'm glad about it
(I'm so glad), I'm glad about it.

(You know he woke me up this morning and I'm glad),
glad),
I'm so glad to be here.

(You know I've got my health and strength and
I'm glad),
I'm glad about it,
(I'm so glad), I'm glad about it
(I'm so glad), I'm glad about it.

(You know I've got my health and strength and
I'm glad),
I'm so glad to be here.

(He put food on the table and I'm glad),
I'm glad about it,
(I'm so glad), I'm glad about it
(I'm so glad), I'm glad about it.

(You know he put food on the table and I'm glad),
I'm glad about it, (You know that)
I'm so glad to be here.

I'M
HANGRY

(It's another day's journey and I'm glad)
I'm glad about it,
(I'm glad), I'm glad about it,
(I'm so glad), I'm glad about it.

(It's another day's journey and I'm glad),
I'm glad about it, (You know that)
I'm so glad to be here.

(He gave me a voice to sang with and I'm glad)
I'm glad about it,
(I'm glad), I'm glad about it,
(I'm so glad), I'm glad about it.

(He gave me a voice to sang with and I'm glad),
I'm glad about it, (You know that)
I'm so glad to be here.

Lord you brought me, from a mighty long way.
Lord you kept me. Let me see another day.
In my darkest hour, Lord you stood by me.
Without you Lord I don't know what I would do.

HE IS
RISEN
Faith Covenant Fellowship

(Lord you gave me a choice to serve you and
I'm glad)
I'm glad about it,
(I'm glad), I'm glad about it,
(I'm so glad), I'm glad about it.

(Lord you gave me a choice to serve you and
I'm glad),
I'm glad about it, (You know that)
I'm so glad to be here.

(It's another day's journey and I'm glad)
I'm glad about it,
(I'm glad), I'm glad about it,
(I'm so glad), I'm glad about it.

(It's another day's journey and I'm glad)
I'm glad about it,
Thank you for the holy ghost power!

Thank you for your love, (It's another day's
journey and I'm glad.)

I'm so glad to be here!

Play These Chords

Every young child loves to listen to music, bang on drums, and pound the keys of a piano. Now here's *Jonah's Journey*, A book that can teach kids of all ages about music and the way to sing it, or even play it on the piano. Jonah's Journey is told in clear and easy terms with read-aloud words. This wonderful book featuring bright, cheerful illustrations, makes learning fun for young children. And each page offers helpful prompts for engaging with your children and encouraging them to sing along.

Up and coming author, La'Tosha Price welcomes her new character, "Jonah" into her new series "Jonah's Journey," which appears in her beloved children's book, *"It's Another Day's Journey"* This uplifting sing-along book will encourage young hearts by exploring the glory and design of God's message, and leading children readers towards Him with praise and worship. Through this wonderful, heartfelt series, Jonah's Journey becomes a rhythmic, whimsical journey through songs of praise.

For spiritual parents who are looking for a different kind of spiritual book for your young child, this charming book offers parents an uncomplicated and loving way to bring your little ones closer to God. In "It's Another Day's Journey" your little ones will find themselves in a special world in which they can explore the characteristics of God through song.

La'Tosha was inspired by her son, Jonah, who, at the young age of 8 starting playing the piano by ear and singing songs based on his love of God. La' Tosha realized that Jonah was blessed by God with the voice of an angel, and she needed to create a book based on Jonah's Journey through his love for music and his gift of song.

La'Tosha Price is a Vendor Management Professional. She's a native of Bardstown, Kentucky, married to Carlos Price for twenty-two blissful years, and the proud mother of three daughters and one son. She's also a grandmother. La' Tosha has been honored with the *Positive Leadership Award*, the *Dean's Award* from Spencerian College, and *the President's Club Award* from Beta Sigma Chi Chapter. In her youth, she won a *Young Leader Writing Award*, had her story featured on the front page of the Bardstown newspaper, and received an honorary trip to South Carolina with co-writer Cabrina Logan of Bardstown Kentucky.
La' Tosha and husband Carlos are Assistant Pastors at Faith Covenant Fellowship Church of Winter Park, FL. under the direction of Bishop Barry Brandon. When La' Tosha is not working, she loves to write, swim, participate in theatrical arts, and go bike riding. She and her family reside in Kissimmee, Florida.

www.ingramcontent.com/pod-product-compliance
Lightning Source LLC
Chambersburg PA
CBHW042133110726
48006CB00003B/865